D1093259

To Be A Line

Written and Illustrated by

SARAH OTTS

1540457

Palmetto Publishing Group
Charleston, SC

To Be a Line
Copyright © 2019 by Sarah Otts

Cover design by Hadley Binion Designs
Photo Credit: Janie Long Photography

First Edition

Printed in the United States

ISBN-13: 978-1-64111-333-5
ISBN-10: 1-64111-333-2

DEDICATION

For Lelia, Sonny, and Josephine.

Trust God's design and His voice in your heart.

My love for you goes on and on, growing and growing every day.

Nana

But the question is not what we intended ourselves
to be, but what He intended us to be when He made
us. He is the inventor, we are only the machine. He is
the painter, we are only the picture.

C.S. Lewis, *Mere Christianity*

What is a line, and what can it make?

How does it grow, and what does it take?

What might we learn from an artist who knew

Her heart would guide her hand as she drew?

This is the tale of a line who would grow;

A story of hope every heart ought'a know.

It all began with something quite small. This was not just a dot and not just a speck. This was the exciting moment when . . .

A line was born! You see, a line is a special kind of mark. The possibilities of a line are endless.

A line goes on and on,
growing and growing,
twisting and turning
and creating along
the way.

Oh, how exciting it is to be a line!

As Line grew, he began to notice he was not alone in the world of design. He especially noticed one particular group, the shapes.

Line liked the way the shapes looked, and most of all, he liked the way the shapes looked together. He wanted to be like them, and he wanted to be a part of their group.

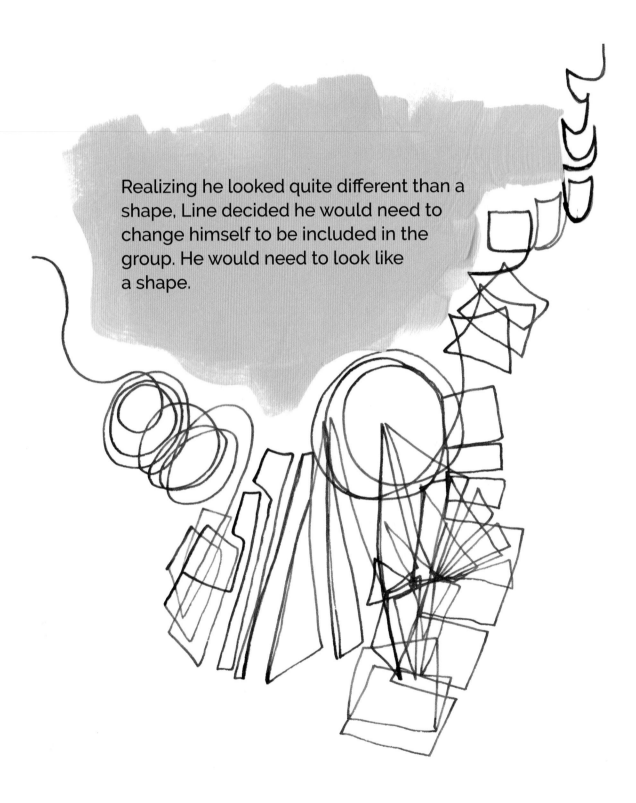

Realizing he looked quite different than a shape, Line decided he would need to change himself to be included in the group. He would need to look like a shape.

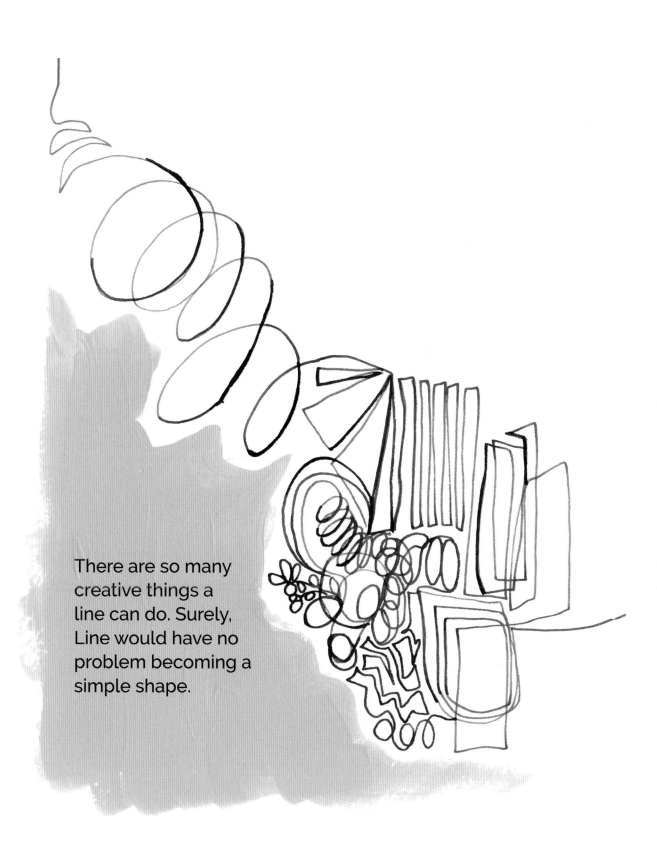

There are so many creative things a line can do. Surely, Line would have no problem becoming a simple shape.

So, he twisted and curled. He went straight and round, up and down, big and small, sharp and soft. . . . He used all of his line tricks until . . . he was all mixed up in a tangled knot. He felt discouraged and downright dizzy, too. Try as he might, Line could not change himself.

By trying to look like someone he was not, Line had drawn himself into quite a confusing picture.

The group of shapes laughed at Line because he did not look like a shape at all, and they left Line out for being too different.

The fact is, while a line is a long mark that goes on and on, a shape is finished and does not keep growing and creating. That's the thing about some folks.

Some of us
were simply made to grow and grow, twisting and turning and creating along the way.

Line felt sad. He tried so hard to be like the shapes, but it was clear that a line is different than a shape.

Line straightened himself out. He sorted through his tangles and knots and went back to being himself: a mark full of possibilities. Although he was hurt, Line chose to do what made him happiest. So, he carried on . . .

. . . and on and on,

growing and growing,

twisting and turning and creating along the way.

Line had been so focused on what he was not meant to be that he almost forgot what he was meant to be!

He almost forgot . . .

oh, how exciting it is

to be a line!

Line twisted and curled. He went straight and round, up and down, winding in and out and all about. He took up all of the space he needed, creating something only a line can create.

Line felt proud. He was truly happy, and it showed.
By simply being himself, Line was growing far past a
shape. Line was becoming a drawing!

Then, Line began to wonder . . .
What else could he grow
and become?

Oh, the possibilities!

When the shapes saw Line and the spectacular drawing he had become, they were jealous. They liked the way Line looked now. This time around, the shapes wanted to be like Line.

The group said to Line, "We want to change ourselves to become an exciting drawing just like you!"

Line had not forgotten how the shapes treated him before, but Line determined no one should be left out for being different.

Line explained to the shapes, "Do you remember when I wanted to be a shape, too? I liked the way you all looked together, but when I tried to be like you, I wasn't being myself."

Line continued, "See, you all have endings and edges and corners, where I am a mark that grows on and on. We are different designs. You cannot be a line drawing, and I cannot be a simple shape. But I have an idea that will include all of your shapes *and* my line."

So Line and the shapes went to work. Instead of leaving the shapes out for being different, Line found a way for them to work together.

What Line and the shapes created was more than a drawing. It was more than a set of shapes . . .

It was a unique work
of art!

What is a line, and what can it make?
How does it grow, and what does it take?
What did you learn from the shapes and a line?
Everyone's different and one of a kind.
This is the tale of a line who would grow,
A story of hope every heart ought'a know.

What makes you different sets you apart.
It's what makes you special.
It's what makes your mark.
You are you by design.
Trust in your heart,
And grow like a line.

AUTHOR BIOGRAPHY

As a full-time artist, Sarah Otts has spent the majority of her life with a paintbrush in hand. In 2007, she graduated from The University of Mississippi, where she acquired a BFA with an emphasis in painting. Otts returned to her hometown, Mobile, Alabama, anxious to start the art career she had long since anticipated. She is currently living in Mobile with her husband, Robert, and their three children, Lelia, Sonny, and Josephine. Otts continues to paint full time in her home studio. In addition to drawing and painting, writing became an additional form of expression and a key component to her creative process, which she describes as "allowing my hand and heart to work together."

Painting has given me the lucidity to hear my heart and know some clear and refreshing truths. Through art, I came to know my truest self. I learned to trust the tugs in my heart that gently guide me down the path God has set me on.

I teach my children we were all created by God to be the very person we are, but I want to help them better understand this concept at their young age. This book is a simple yet whimsical representation of the freedom that comes with trusting your heart. There is great satisfaction in discovering true purpose and letting it grow. Line teaches us what it takes to make your mark.

For more information about
Sarah Otts go to
www.sarahotts.com